Adapted by Kiki Thorpe

Based on the series created by

Mark McCorkle & Bob Schooley

Watch it on

Disney CHANNEL

abc Kids

Disney PRESS

VOLO

New York

Printed in the United States of America

First Edition
3 5 7 9 10 8 6 4 2

Library of Congress Catalog Card Number: 2002095025

ISBN 0-7868-4481-7
For more Disney Press fun, visit www.disneybooks.com
Visit DisneyChannel.com

CHAPTER 1

Drakken's Back!

"It's criminal!" Kim Possible cried.

Kim stared at an ugly, baby-blue jacket on the screen of her Kimmunicator. The Kimmunicator was like a walkie-talkie combined with a high-speed computer. Kim used it to get information from all over the world. Even the latest catalog from her favorite store, Club Banana.

Kim pushed a button to flip through the catalog. Different coats appeared on-screen.

A boxy blue jacket with a zipper—*ugh*. A long wool overcoat—*as if*. A fluffy pink coat with big buttons. Kim wrinkled her nose.

"Someone at Club Banana is in major style denial," she said.

Just then, Kim spotted a green leather jacket with a belt around the waist. The jacket matched Kim's green eyes perfectly.

"Now, *this* is me," she said. "Come to Kim."

Suddenly, the coat disappeared from the screen. Her friend Wade's face appeared instead.

"I have bad news," Wade told Kim.

Kim slumped in her beanbag chair. "No kidding," she said, pouting. "I *cannot* afford that jacket."

"I know," Wade said. "I looked at your bank account. You're broke. But that's not the bad news."

Wade ran Kim's Website. Even though he was only ten years old, Wade was a supergenius. He was also supernosy.

"Apparently, the bad news is that you've been hacking into my account," she said. Suddenly, a horrible thought crossed her mind. "Have you peeked at my diary?" she asked.

"Of course not," Wade said. "Anyway, the bad news is that Drakken has escaped from prison."

A mug shot of Drakken, the mad scientist, flashed onto the screen. Drakken had blue skin and black hair. A long scar ran down his left cheek. His face could have scared Frankenstein.

But Drakken wasn't just ugly. He was evil.

Drakken

Drakken and his assistant, Shego, were determined to take over the world. Kim had stopped them once. And it looked like she was going to have to stop them again.

At the beginning of her sophomore year, Kim had posted a message on her Website that said, "I can do anything." Kim was hoping she'd get a job baby-sitting. Or maybe walking dogs. Instead, Kim got messages from people all over the world asking for help—serious help. Fighting-sinister-badguys kind of help. Pretty soon Kim realized that she really *could* do anything. Now when she wasn't in school or at cheerleading practice, Kim saved lives and captured evil criminals.

Kim stared at Drakken's hideous picture. "That's major bad," she said.

"Almost as bad as last week at school— when you used the boys' room by accident," Wade said.

"Nobody saw that—" Kim started to say.

Shego

Suddenly, she gasped. "You *have* been reading my diary!"

"Good luck on the mission! Bye!" Wade said quickly. Before Kim could say another word, the Kimmunicator screen went blank.

CHAPTER 2

Snow Trouble

Sporting a red fleece jacket, a helmet, and goggles, Kim raced across the Alaskan tundra on a dogsled. The huskies pulling the sled barked and panted as they charged through the snow.

Kim's best friend, Ron Stoppable, sat in the front of the sled. His pet, Rufus, rode in his coat pocket. Ron was a tall, skinny boy with freckles. Rufus was a small, pink naked mole rat with big teeth. Both of them were shivering.

Akut, the Alaskan man who owned the dogsled, sat behind Kim. Kim wasn't old enough to drive, so she had to ask her friends from around the world for a ride whenever she needed one.

Suddenly, a shout came from the front of the sled. "Kim!" Ron cried. "I'm snow-blind!"

Kim casually reached forward and wiped the snow off Ron's goggles.

"Ron," she scolded, "you're supposed to be looking for signs of Drakken."

Earlier that day, an oil rig near the Alaskan pipeline had mysteriously disappeared. Kim thought Drakken might be

behind it. She'd come to Alaska to look for clues.

As their sled got to the top of a hill, they saw a huge oil drilling rig below them. Four helicopters hovered in the sky above it.

Ron pushed his goggles up. "Okay," he said, pointing. "That looks suspicious."

Kim rolled her eyes. "Thank you, Captain Obvious," she said. "Keep your eyes open for any—"

ROARRRRR! A loud engine drowned out Kim's voice. A girl on a snowmobile flew over the top of the hill and raced up next to the dogsled. Her long black hair whipped in the wind.

"Shego!" Ron cried. "The mad scientist's mad assistant."

Zipping past Kim and Ron's sled, Shego yelled, "Bye-bye!" She threw a handful of dog treats into the snow. The sled lurched to a halt as the huskies stopped to gobble up the treats.

Quickly, Kim clamped a snowboard onto her boots and chased after Shego.

Ron tried to put on his snowboard, but he lost his balance. He fell face first into the snow.

Rufus tumbled out of Ron's pocket. He rolled to a stop right in front of a dog treat.

"*Mmm,*" Rufus said, grabbing the treat.

"Don't eat it, Rufus," Ron warned. "It could be—"

Rufus stuffed the treat into Ron's mouth.

"*Mmm*," Ron said, chewing. "Bacon-y."

Meanwhile, Kim was racing down a steep slope. Shego was only a few feet ahead of her.

Now that she was close enough, Kim noticed that Shego was wearing a leather jacket. It was just like the one she'd seen in the Club Banana catalog. Only Shego's was black.

"Nice jacket!" Kim called out. "Club Banana?"

"The very latest," Shego shouted back proudly.

"Get a new lifestyle, Shego," Kim said. "Green is the new black."

Shego glared at Kim. "And this advice comes from a 'fashion don't' in fleece," she replied. Laughing, she stepped on the gas and zoomed away.

Kim looked down at her own red fleece jacket. Fleece was perfectly acceptable in the snow, wasn't it? Kim thought. Then she scowled and raced after Shego.

The drilling rig was just ahead of them. But as Kim watched, the giant rig suddenly rose off the ground. The helicopters were lifting it into the air!

Shego slowed down for a second and turned to show Kim what she had in her hand—a bomb!

"It's going to blow the pipeline, Kimmie," said Shego. "And your skin definitely doesn't need more oil."

With a wicked laugh, Shego slapped the bomb onto the front of her snowmobile. Then she drove the snowmobile straight at the oil pipeline.

Just as she reached the drilling rig, Shego leaped off the snowmobile. She grabbed the bottom of the oil rig as it rose into the air.

Now Shego was completely out of Kim's reach. As the rig flew higher, Kim spotted Drakken on it. He was waving at her mockingly.

On the ground, Kim tore after the snow-mobile. The bomb was set to explode in fifteen seconds. If it hit the pipeline, it would blow up half of Alaska!

When she was close enough, Kim took a flying leap off her snowboard. She landed on the snowmobile. Grabbing the handles, she steered the snowmobile away from the pipeline.

The snowmobile sped over a jump and soared through the air. At the last second, Kim leaped off. The snowmobile exploded in the air above her. Kim skidded to a stop at the edge of a cliff.

Stopping to catch her breath, Kim heard someone call her name.

"Here I come, K.P.!" Ron hollered. He slid down the hill on his snowboard, his arms flailing wildly. He was totally out of control!

Kim knew what was coming next. She turned her head so she wouldn't have to watch.

Wham! Ron and Rufus smacked into the pipeline.

Ooof! They fell back into the snow.

Kim looked up into the sky. The drilling rig was a dot in the distance.

Drakken had escaped.

CHAPTER 3

Bueno Whatcho?

The next morning, Kim woke up early. She was feeling a little bummed about Drakken getting away, but she was really bummed that she couldn't afford the cool jacket she wanted. There had to be a way she could get it, so she gave herself a special assignment for the day. Mission: get the Club Banana jacket.

"Morning, Dad," Kim said as she sat down at the breakfast table. She set the Club

Banana catalog down next to her bowl of cereal.

Kim's dad, Dr. Possible, the rocket scientist, looked up from the blueprints he had laid out on the table. He was working on a design for a new rocket.

"Good morning," he said. "How's my teen hero?"

"Moderately bummed," Kim said. "Drakken got away."

"Well, I'm sure you'll get him next time," Kim's dad said absently. He turned back to his drawing, muttering, "Now these launch vectors are all wrong. . . ."

Kim slid the Club Banana catalog over her dad's rocket drawing. She pointed at the picture of the green leather jacket.

"Dad, what do you think of this jacket?" she asked. "For me. Just because."

Kim stuck her bottom lip out in an adorable pout. She looked at her father with puppy-dog eyes.

Kim's dad looked at the jacket. Then he looked at the price of the jacket. He frowned.

"Don't you already have a functional coat?" he asked.

Kim stopped pouting and rolled her eyes.

"My jacket's from *last season*," she told him. "It's *red*."

"Didn't you say red was the new black?" her dad asked.

"Red's dead, Dad," Kim said. Her father was *so* unhip. "*Green* is the new black."

Just then Jim and Tim, Kim's twin brothers, rushed into the room.

As usual, they're up to something, Kim thought.

"Dad!" they shouted.

Kim glared at them. "Jim. Tim. I'm working here," she said.

Jim and Tim glared back. "So are we," Jim said.

"What's the combustion temperature of the J-200 fuel you developed?" Tim asked their father.

"Forty-seven degrees Celsius, Tim," Dr. Possible answered. "Why?"

Jim and Tim looked at each other nervously. "No special reason," said Jim.

Suddenly—*KA-BOOM!* —a loud explosion rocked the house.

"Gotta go!" Jim and Tim cried, dashing out of the room.

Ignoring the explosion, Kim's father turned his attention back to his daughter.

"You know, Kim," he said. "Your problem

reminds me of the time I asked for money for a new propulsion system. The university told me money doesn't grow on trees."

Kim sighed loudly. She put her head down on the table. She'd heard this story, like, a million times before.

"I told them, money is made of paper," Dr. Possible went on. "And paper comes from trees. So, in fact, money does grow on trees."

Kim looked up at her dad.

"And this relates to me how?" she asked.

"Not sure exactly," he said, scratching his head. "But no new jacket."

Just then, Kim's mom, Dr. Possible, the brain surgeon, walked into the kitchen. She was wearing her white doctor's coat and carrying a newspaper.

"Morning, Kimmie," she said. She kissed Kim's cheek. Then she noticed the Club Banana catalog. "Cute jacket," she said.

"Thank you!" Kim exclaimed happily. "Can you explain that to Dad, who incorrectly believes that I don't need it?"

"Sorry, baby. I'm due at the hospital," Kim's mom said. "But if you *need* it, I have a suggestion."

She held up a newspaper ad for

Bueno Nacho, the local Mexican restaurant and one of Kim and Ron's favorite hangouts.  Beneath the picture, it said HELP WANTED in big red letters.

"A job?" Kim stuck out her tongue. "At Bueno Nacho?" Was her mother serious?

"Now that's the way forward," her dad said cheerfully.

Kim slumped down in her seat, defeated. "Between a rocket scientist and a brain surgeon, the best idea you can come up with is minimum wage?" she asked.

Her mom shrugged. "You practically live there, anyway," she said.

"Come on, Ron," Kim begged. "We practically live here, anyway."

They were sitting in a booth at Bueno

Nacho. As Kim filled out a job application, Ron munched on some nachos.

"Kim, never work where you food," Ron said. He tossed a nacho chip into the air and caught it in his mouth.

Frustrated, Kim said, "It's the only way. The 'rents were totally neg on just buying me the jacket."

"Did you try the puppy-dog pout?" Ron asked.

"No effect," Kim said sadly. "If I want the jacket, I have to earn it."

"Harsh," said Ron. He picked up the nachos and dumped them into a taco shell.

Melted cheese and taco sauce oozed out the sides.

Kim stared at the dripping mess. "What are you eating?" she asked.

"Taco meets nacho," Ron said proudly, displaying his handiwork to Kim. "I call it 'The Naco.'"

"I call it 'Gross Beyond Reason,'" Kim said.

Ron took a huge bite of his Naco. "You want some?" he asked with his mouth full.

Kim wrinkled her nose. Just then, Rufus popped out of Ron's pocket. His eyes lit up when he saw the Naco. He started to smack his lips and rub his tummy.

25

Kim glared at Ron. "You know, restaurants don't exactly welcome pets," she said.

"Rufus isn't a pet," Ron said matter-of-factly. "He's family."

"The *rodent* family," Kim said.

Ron picked Rufus up and put him back in his pocket.

"Sorry, buddy," he said, patting his little friend's head.

Kim looked at the picture of the jacket in the Club Banana catalog.

"I did the math," she told Ron. "Two weeks of drudge work and I'm in green leather."

Kim was snapped out of her Club Banana fog when she heard someone calling her name.

"Miss Possible?" said a boy standing next to their booth.

Kim and Ron looked up. The boy was wearing a green-and-orange Bueno Nacho shirt and a necktie. He had greasy hair and pimply skin. In his hands he held a clipboard.

"I'm Ned, assistant manager here at Bueno Nacho number five eighty-two," he said in a whiny voice.

"Hola, amigo," Kim said. She gave him a big, toothpaste-commercial smile.

Ned didn't smile back. "Your bilingual wiles will hold no sway with me, Ms. Possible," he said. "I am Management."

He picked up Kim's application and looked at it carefully. Ron made goofy faces behind his back.

Ned looked up. Ron stopped making faces just in time. He gave Ned a big smile.

"Is that a clip-on tie, Ned?" Ron asked brightly.

Ned nodded. "For quick removal in the event of a grease fire," he explained, popping the tie off and on. Then he turned to Kim and asked, "When can you start?"

"Born ready, sir," Kim replied.

Ned looked at another form. "And you?" he asked Ron.

"Me, what?" said Ron.

"Isn't this your application, Mr. Stoppable?" Ned asked. He held up a piece of paper.

Ron glared at Kim.

"You didn't!" he cried.

Kim stuck her bottom lip out and looked at Ron with puppy-dog eyes.

"It'll be more fun if we *both* work here," she said sweetly.

"Oh, no!" Ron cried, defeated. "Not the puppy-dog pout!"

Kim smiled. Her parents might be immune to it, but it got Ron every time.

CHAPTER 4

Nacho Blues

That afternoon, Kim and Ron stood behind the counter at Bueno Nacho looking stunned. They wore stiff green-and-white polyester shirts and Bueno Nacho baseball caps.

Ned handed each of them a fat notebook.

"Bueno Nacho S.O.P.," he said.

"Excuse me?" Kim asked, weighed down by the stack of papers.

"Standard operating procedures," Ned explained. "Learn them. Know them. Live them."

Ron shot Kim a dirty look. He leaned in closer and growled, "I'm going to get you for this."

Kim closed her eyes and pretended she couldn't hear him. "Two weeks to jacket . . . two weeks to jacket," she sang.

Ned wasted no time getting his new employees trained. Their first lesson was the Combo Plate. As Kim plopped refried beans and salsa onto a paper plate, Ned watched over her shoulder.

"Not enough lettuce. Too much salsa," he snapped. "And don't get me started on those beans."

He pointed at Ron's plate. "Notice how he sculpts the frijoles, evoking the majesty of a Mayan temple," Ned said.

Happily surprised, Ron said, "Really? Ya think?" He admired his beans, which really *did* look sort of like a Mayan temple.

"You're ready for burrito folding," Ned told him.

"Right on," Ron said proudly.

At the burrito counter, Ron swiftly folded beans and cheese into a perfect airtight package. He held it up to show Ned.

Ned smiled approvingly and made a note on his clipboard. Then he turned to Kim.

Kim held her burrito up for inspection, but the end came unfolded. Beans and cheese oozed onto the counter.

Ned gave her a disappointed look.

"Possible, I'm putting you on cheese duty," he said. "Even *you* can push a button."

Ned led Kim over to the cheese machine. He pushed a button. Liquid cheese squirted over a pile of tortilla chips.

Ned held the cheesy chips under Kim's nose.

"Think you can handle this?" he asked.

Kim sighed. "Mission: possible," she said.

As Ned walked away, Kim ripped the picture of her jacket out of the Club Banana catalog and taped it to the cheese machine.

"I can get through this," she told herself. "Two weeks to jacket . . . two weeks to jacket . . ."

Suddenly, Kim's Kimmunicator beeped.

"What up, Wade?" she asked, pulling it out of her pocket.

"I've scanned all recent satellite photos," he said. "But there's no sign of the stolen laser drill."

Kim frowned. "It must be hidden," she said.

Suddenly, a shadow fell across the Kimmunicator. Kim looked up. Ned stood before her, looking unhappy.

"Playing video games on the job is not S.O.P.," he whined. "I'm docking your pay an hour."

So unfair, Kim thought. Try to do the

world a favor and get docked an hour's pay.

On the other side of the room, Ron was single-handedly running both the burrito station and the taco salad station. With one hand, he dumped lettuce into taco shells. With the other, he folded burritos into origami masterpieces.

"Multitasking?" Ned asked. "Excellent, Stoppable."

"Just doing my job, Ned," said Ron.

As Ned walked off to inspect the deep fryer, Kim shot a look at Ron.

"Hello? Kim to Ron!" she cried. "You didn't even *want* this job!"

"I didn't know what I wanted, Kim," Ron

said, looking off into space. "I was lost. Adrift in the wilderness. But that was then."

Ron leaned closer to Kim. There were tears in his eyes.

"Now I belong," Ron said, clutching his hand to his heart. "I belong to Bueno Nacho!"

Whirling around, Ron strode over to the door. He threw it open and hollered out to the world.

"*Te amo este lugar!*" he shouted. "I love this place!"

Rufus popped up from Ron's pocket.

"*Sí!*" he squeaked.

CHAPTER 5

So Long, Ron

Bueno Nacho had never seen an employee like Ron. He worked like a machine, scooping beans, squirting hot sauce, and wrapping burritos. His perfect Combo Plates didn't have so much as a stray drip of salsa.

Ron enjoyed adding personal little touches to his job. "Fifty-eight, your order's great," he sang into the microphone. "Fifty-nine, lookin' fine. Sixty . . . uh, your order's ready."

Standing at the cheese machine, Kim was

steaming. They'd only been working for two days, and already Ron had turned into some kind of Bueno maniac.

Suddenly, her Kimmunicator beeped. Kim pulled it out of her pocket.

"Go, Wade," she said.

"Check this out," Wade said, slurping soda from a supersize takeout cup. "Highly unusual—"

Suddenly, Ron reached over and shut down the Kimmunicator. The screen went blank.

"What are you doing?" Kim asked.

Ron rapped his knuckles on the cheese machine.

"Ix-nay on the Kimmunicator," he said. "The nacho cheese needs some love."

Kim was at a loss for words. What was going on with Ron?

"We might have a lead on Drakken," Kim said. "Drakken . . . nachos . . ." Kim held up her hands as if she were balancing a scale. "I'm gonna have to go with Drakken."

"Well," Ron snapped, "that kind of 'tude is narrowing the race for Employee of the Month."

Kim stared at him in disbelief.

"The race is between *you* and *you*," she snapped back.

Ron huffed angrily and turned his back to Kim. Kim huffed angrily and turned her back to Ron.

"Sometimes I feel like I don't even know you anymore," they said at the same time.

They turned and glared at each other. Not having anything more to say, they both stomped off.

As Ron walked away, Rufus popped out of his pocket. Kim spied him.

"Ru-fus . . ." she called sweetly. "Che-ese!"

She waved a cheesy tortilla chip in the air.

Rufus sniffed at the air. His eyes widened. He leaped out of Ron's pocket, scampered over to Kim, and gobbled up the chip.

"Want more?" she asked.

Rufus smacked his lips.

Kim pushed the button on the cheese machine. Cheese oozed over a pile of chips.

"Even you can push a button, right?" she said to Rufus.

Rufus nodded. He hit the button with his paw. Cheese squirted down. Rufus grabbed a chip off the top of the pile and pushed the rest along the counter.

"Good little naked mole rat," Kim said, patting his head.

With Rufus on cheese duty, Kim turned back to her Kimmunicator and contacted Wade.

"Sorry, Wade," she said. "The Employee of the Month cut us off."

"Seismic activity . . . in Wisconsin," Wade told her.

A map of the United States appeared on the Kimmunicator screen. Red circles indicating an earthquake radiated from the state of Wisconsin.

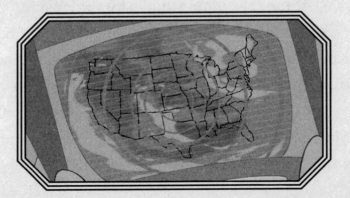

"Quake in the Midwest?" Kim asked, slightly confused. "Major red flag."

"It gets weirder," Wade told her. "The epicenter is the world's biggest cheese wheel."

Kim stared at the map. Suddenly, she had an idea.

"Let me try something," she told Wade.

Kim quickly punched the keys of the Kimmunicator, searching through police files from the Midwest.

"Police report from the Cheese Wheel Mall shows a break-in at the Club Banana store," she reported back to Wade.

Wade shook his head. "I don't get the connection," he said.

"Only one thing was stolen," Kim explained. "A leather jacket."

Kim's brow furrowed as she put the pieces together.

"Shego," she murmured.

Shutting off the Kimmunicator, Kim hurried over to Ned.

"Ned, I've gotta switch shifts," she said. "Something suddenly came up."

"Whatever," Ned said glumly.

Kim eyed him suspiciously. Where was the work responsibility talk she expected? "What's with you?" she asked.

"Go ask your new boss," Ned replied, jerking his thumb toward Ron.

"New boss?" Kim asked, surprised. Suddenly, Kim realized that Ron was wearing a green-and-orange Bueno Nacho manager's shirt—with a clip-on tie!

Kim approached Ron and gave him a look.

"Corporate loved the Naco," Ron explained, tugging on his new tie.

"Oh, really?" Kim said.

"They see big things in my future," Ron said, grinning smugly.

"Good for you," said Kim matter-of-factly. "Now let's go. Drakken's in Wisconsin."

Ron hesitated. "B-but your shift isn't over," he said.

"Ron," Kim said angrily, "an evil wacko is

in the Dairy State with a giant laser drill. I'm going. And I was hoping you'd come with me."

Ron glared at Kim. Their faces were inches apart.

"To be your *sidekick*?" he asked. "That's what this is all about, isn't it? You just can't stand that I'm better than you at something."

Kim couldn't believe what she was hearing. "You wouldn't even have this stupid job if I didn't fill out your application!" she yelled.

"Kim, we could argue all day, but that's not gonna get this floor mopped," Ron said, pointing to a bucket and mop in the corner.

Kim had had enough. She grabbed the mop and shoved it into Ron's hands.

"Mop it yourself, *boss*," she said furiously. She jumped over the counter and strode toward the door. "And find yourself a new nacho drone. I quit," she said, storming out of the restaurant.

"Yeah? Well, find a new sidekick!" Ron yelled at the closed door.

Of course, Ned was close by and overheard everything.

"What are you looking at?" Ron asked him. He shoved the mop into Ned's hands. "I want that floor to sparkle!"

CHAPTER 6

The World's Largest Cheese Wheel

Kim sat in the passenger seat of a crop-dusting plane. Her red hair flapped beneath her aviator cap as she soared over Wisconsin.

"Get ready!" the pilot shouted. "Now!"

The plane rolled over, and Kim dropped from her seat. Hundreds of feet above the ground, she yanked the cord on her parachute. The chute opened and Kim glided down to earth gracefully.

She landed on top of the biggest wheel of

Swiss cheese she had ever seen. It was at least seven stories high and as wide as a city block. A small wedge was cut out of one side. A little monorail tram ran all the way around the giant wheel.

Kim sniffed at the surface and pulled off a chunk of cheese.

"Funky," she said. "A cheese-covered building."

Just then, she heard the monorail approaching.

"Many people assume that this is a cheese-covered building," a tour guide announced to a group of tourists riding the monorail.

Kim ducked into one of the Swiss cheese holes and listened.

"In fact," the tour guide continued, "this marvel of dairy product architecture is one-hundred-percent pure Wisconsin Swiss."

"Ooooh!" the tourists said in unison.

As the monorail passed, Kim suddenly realized that the cheese hole she was hiding in was actually a tunnel! She followed the tunnel, crawling deeper and deeper into the center of the giant cheese.

At last, she saw an opening. Kim crept to the edge and peered out.

The tunnel opened into a giant cavern hidden deep within the cheese wheel. Hundreds of feet below on the cavern floor, Kim saw

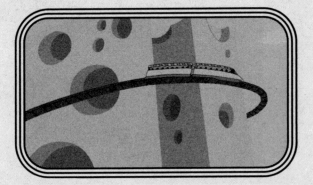

Drakken's oil drilling rig. She had found his secret lair!

Kim looked around, somehow impressed by his choice of location. "Okay, points for a bizarre hiding place," she murmured to herself. She ducked back into the cheese and radioed Wade.

"Wade, get this," she whispered into her Kimmunicator. "I'm inside the cheese wheel."

"Which, surprisingly, is not a cheese-covered building," Wade said knowingly. "It's one-hundred-percent pure Wisconsin Swiss."

"So I've heard," Kim replied. "Drakken's got the whole mad scientist's lair thing here. They love the high ceilings."

"Kim, look in your pack," Wade said, taking a sip of his soda.

Kim dug into her backpack and pulled out a red hair dryer.

"A hair dryer?" she asked, confused.

"It only *looks* like a hair dryer," said Wade.

Kim flipped the power switch. Instantly, a grappling hook popped out from the nozzle of the dryer.

Kim grinned. "You rock, Wade," she said.

Aiming high up on the wall of the cavern, Kim fired the hook. *Thwack!* The steel hook plunged deep into the cheese. Quickly, Kim climbed down the wall.

Once on the cavern floor, Kim tried to stay

out of sight. Hearing Drakken, she ducked behind a large crate.

"Increase the drill's power!" Drakken shouted. "I want to reach that magma!"

Kim was just about to sneak out, when she heard someone say, "Welcome, Kimmie."

Kim spun around. There stood Shego, wearing the Club Banana jacket. On either side of her stood two huge henchmen carrying lasers.

"May I take your coat?" Shego purred.

"You already did," Kim said. "Don't

worry. It'll look better on me."

Springing forward, Kim knocked Shego to the ground. The henchmen rushed at her from either side, but Kim kicked her legs out in a wide split, knocking them both to the ground. She somersaulted forward, overthrowing a third henchman. Scrambling to her feet, she turned to run.

But ten more henchmen blocked her path. She spun around, looking for another way out. But Shego and the other henchmen were behind her. She was trapped!

Shego smiled. Her dark eyes gleamed.

"Face it, pumpkin," she said. "Fashion isn't the only thing in which I'm a step ahead."

As Kim glared at her, the henchmen closed in.

CHAPTER 7

Drakken's Evil Plan

Kim struggled, but it was no use. The henchmen held her tight. They drove her up against a giant slab of metal.

Shego pushed a button. *Clank! Clank!* Iron shackles emerged from the metal slab. They clamped around Kim's wrists and ankles.

"Comfy?" Shego asked sarcastically.

Kim gave her a look. "Not particularly," she said.

"Good," Shego said with an evil smile.

54

Suddenly, a trapdoor opened right in front of Kim. Drakken rose up from the floor.

"Well, well," he said, chuckling. "Kim Possible. How nice to see you again. Especially now that you're helpless to stop me."

Rubbing his hands together excitedly, Drakken leaned in close to Kim. "Shall I tell you my plan?" he asked. "It's quite impressive."

Kim wrinkled her nose. Drakken's breath was terrible.

Without missing a beat, Kim said, "You're using the world's most powerful laser drill to tap into the molten magma deep beneath the earth's crust."

Drakken blinked, annoyed. Kim had foiled his chance to reveal his evil plot. He was speechless for a moment.

"Ah!" he cried at last. "That's Phase One. In Phase Two, which you did not guess, my Magmamachine will melt the entire state of Wisconsin. Which I will then rebuild and rename Drakkenville!"

"You're so conceited," Kim said, shrugging him off.

Drakken smiled. "I'll take that as a compliment," he replied.

Then he impatiently walked over to the laser drill and shouted, "Shego! How long?"

High up in the cab of the drill, Shego was working the controls. She looked at a gauge showing a graphic readout of the drill's descent through the earth's crust. It had nearly reached the magma.

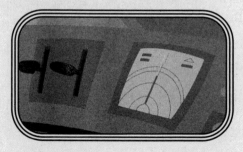

"The alarm will go off when we hit magma," she said.

"You see?"

Drakken crowed to Kim. "Any second now I will strike swiftly and without mercy."

"Actually," Shego called out. "Make it more like half an hour."

Drakken scowled. "Fine. Whatever," he said, annoyed. "In roughly thirty minutes, Wisconsin will be a smoldering memory, and the kingdom of Drakkenville will be born!"

He reached out and squeezed Kim's cheeks. "Say it with me—Drak-ken-ville." Drakken cackled evilly. "Doesn't that have a nice ring?" he asked.

CHAPTER 8

Ron to the Rescue

Standing by the drive-through window, Ron shouted over to Ned. "Step it up! These customers have been waiting for over thirty seconds." He held up a stopwatch. "Thirty-three! Thirty-four!" he counted. *"Andale."*

Ned finished stuffing tacos into a paper bag. He hurried over to the drive-through window and handed the bag to a waiting customer.

"Have a *muy bueno* day," Ned said unenthusiastically.

Just then Ron heard a voice on the drive-through headset he was wearing.

"Ron!" the voice said.

"Welcome to Bueno Nacho," Ron said into the headset. "May I take your order?"

"Ron, it's *Wade*."

"Wade?" Ron said in surprise.

Ron stuck his head out the drive-through window. Wade was nowhere in sight.

"Where are you?" he asked.

"Not important," Wade told him. "Kim's in trouble. She found Drakken inside a giant cheese wheel. But I lost contact with her. She needs help. *Your* help."

"Well, well, well," Ron heard someone say in his other ear.

He turned. Ned was standing right behind him. He had heard everything.

"Looks like you've got a choice to make, Stoppable," Ned snarled. "What's more important? Your sacred duty as assistant manager? Or your pathetic role as goofy sidekick?"

Ned's eyes narrowed. Ron's lip curled back from his teeth.

"Well," Ron said at last, "that's no choice at all. I guess it's time to say *buenos noches*, Bueno Nacho."

Ron leaped over the counter and rushed out the door to save Kim.

A short time later, Ron was in Wisconsin, riding the cheese wheel monorail with the other tourists.

"Question!" Ron called out to the tour

guide. "Is this some kind of cheese-covered building?"

The tour guide chuckled. "You know, you'd be surprised at how many people think that," she said.

Inside Drakken's lair, Kim was still pinned to the metal slab. Drakken laughed as she struggled against the iron shackles.

"Don't bother." He sneered. "The Midwest is about to receive a molten calling card from a certain Dr. Drakken."

Drakken looked up at the drill's cab where Shego was still busy at the controls.

"Shego!" he shouted. "I'm waiting."

"So, read a magazine," Shego snapped. "I'm working."

"Excuse me," he said to Kim. "I have to go make a scene." Scowling fiercely, he marched up to the cab.

"Can't you drill any faster?" he shouted at the henchman. "I've built an entire army of evil robots in the time it's taking you to penetrate the earth's crust!"

Just then, Ron made his way into the cheese and tiptoed around the laser drill. He crept up to Kim.

"Ron!" she whispered happily.

"Everything's okay, Kim," he said. "I'm here to save the day!"

But before he could make a move, Ron was grabbed from behind by two henchmen. They turned him around to face Shego. She looked at his Bueno Nacho uniform with disgust.

"Is that a clip-on tie?" she asked.

Ron's face turned red.

"Heh, heh, heh," he laughed nervously. He popped off the tie as Drakken's henchmen shackled him next to Kim.

CHAPTER 9

Magma!

"Guess that wasn't much of a plan," Ron admitted.

"Not as great as your Bueno Nacho bathroom-break chart," Kim replied, annoyed.

Ron looked at her sheepishly. "I gooned on Assistant Manager power. You were right," he said.

Kim hung her head. She didn't want to have to say it, but felt she had to. "I did resent your superior burrito technique," she

admitted. "You're entitled to excel. Forgive me?" she asked.

"Duh," said Ron. "Forgive me?"

Kim grinned. She could never stay mad at Ron.

"Totally," she said.

Just then, a dark shadow fell over them. Drakken had returned!

"Aww . . . that's so sweet," the mad scientist said mockingly. "Friends again. Just in time to be fried in magma!"

Ron gulped and looked at Kim.

"Remind me again why I rushed over?" he said.

At that moment, the drill's beam cut through the last layer of the earth's crust. It splashed down into a sea of molten rock.

"The drill's into the magma!" Shego cried out to Drakken.

"About time!" he said. "Activate the Magmamachine!"

Shego hit a few buttons on the control panel. The laser beam shut down. Slowly, the giant laser drill moved to the side of the cavern.

In its place, a monstrous machine moved over to the hole. Kim and Ron watched in horror as one end of the machine slammed down over the magma hole.

"That would be so cool if it weren't going to hurt us," Ron whimpered.

"Show time!" Drakken roared, smiling at last. "Deploy the barrel and activate the magma pump!"

One of his henchmen turned a dial on the control panel. The top of the machine opened and a huge, telescoping barrel shot upward. It grew longer and longer until it punched through the top of the cheese wheel!

Chunks of Swiss flew into the air. More rained down around the monorail.

Deep inside the cheese wheel, the Magmamachine began to suck magma up from the center of the earth. Kim gasped. In only a few minutes, the cannon would spray fiery magma over the entire state of Wisconsin. They were almost out of time!

Yawning sleepily, Rufus poked his head out of Ron's pocket. He'd been napping the whole time.

Kim's face lit up when she saw him.

"Rufus!" she said. She motioned toward the button that activated the shackles. "Push the button."

Rufus looked up at the button. Remembering the cheese machine at Bueno Nacho, he scurried over to the button. But he couldn't reach it. He tried once . . . twice . . .

Kim and Ron held their breath.

Suddenly, Rufus threw himself against the button. The shackles released. Kim and Ron fell to the floor. Rufus landed on Ron's head. Quick as a wink, they scrambled to their feet and dashed away.

CHAPTER 10

The Big Cheese-y

Ron and Kim crept around the base of the giant laser drill, looking for a way to stop the Magmamachine. Drakken and Shego were busy aiming the machine's cannon at Milwaukee. They didn't notice that Kim and Ron were gone.

"Ron! Get to the laser drill," Kim said. "I'll take care of Shego."

"Great plan!" said Ron.

He took one step. Then he stopped and looked back at Kim.

"What exactly is the plan again?" he asked.

"Ron, you're the genius who invented the Naco," Kim said. "You've got a building made of cheese here. Get creative."

Ron grinned.

"It will be my masterpiece," he said.

"Be careful!" Kim and Ron said at the same time.

"Jinx, you owe me a soda," Kim said. She winked and dashed away.

Just then, Drakken glimpsed her out of the corner of his eye. He turned and saw the empty shackles.

"They've escaped!" Drakken cried.

"No. Really?" Shego said sarcastically.

"The buffoon is nothing," Drakken said as Shego started after them. "Find Kim Possible!"

Quickly, Kim leaped up a stack of crates. At the top, she stopped to catch her breath. Suddenly Shego soared over Kim's head. She landed in front of Kim. Her hands crackled with green electricity.

"Lesson time, princess," Shego hissed.

"With that trendy coat weighing you down? I'm thinking not," Kim said.

Shego lunged at Kim with a flying kick. Kim tumbled out of the way at the last second. Shego flew past her and landed on her feet. She whirled around and came at Kim again. Kim ducked and spun, blocking Shego's blows with karate chops and cheerleading kicks.

Shego was furious. With a fierce growl, she lunged forward and threw a mighty punch.

Kim stepped out of the way. Shego's hand smashed through a wooden crate.

She spun around and faced Kim again, her eyes glowing with anger.

Meanwhile, Drakken was at the controls of the Magmamachine.

"Here comes the magma!" he cried, cackling evilly. He didn't notice Ron climbing the ladder to the laser drill's cab.

Ron pulled the cab door shut behind him. He stared at the blinking lights, keys, and dials on the drill's control panel. Rufus watched from Ron's pocket.

"Rufus, this is a precision instrument.

Incredibly complex," Ron said. He thought for a moment. "Better mess with everything," he said. He began pushing all the buttons and twisting all the dials.

Lights flashed on and off. An alarm shrieked.

"Stop him!" Drakken·screamed.

A group of henchmen ran toward the drill.

In the cab, Ron squinted at the label next to a large lever.

"Angle adjustment?" he read. Shrugging, Ron pushed the lever forward.

The laser cannon tilted up and hit the henchmen. They tumbled every which way.

"Boo-ya!" Ron cried, high-fiving Rufus.

As the laser beam hit the cavern wall, the cheese began to melt. Slowly, the laser

swiveled around. The entire building started to collapse. Gooey, fondue-y cheese flooded the floor of the cavern.

Now, the beam was heading straight for the crate where Kim and Shego were still fighting. Kim looked up just in time. Quickly, she grabbed her hair dryer and fired the hook into the ceiling. Kim leaped. A second later, the laser blasted the wooden crate to bits.

"Ahhh!" Shego screamed. She tumbled through the air and landed in a river of melted Swiss.

Kim swung though the air on the end of her rope. Below her, she saw Ron standing on top of the laser drill, which by now was almost covered in melted cheese. She

swooped down and grabbed him, just before the drill sank into the gooey mess.

Drakken was too busy watching his Magmamachine fill up to notice what was going on. At last, it was full. The lights on the control panel turned green.

"Eat magma, Milwaukee!" Drakken yelled.

He slammed his fist down on the FIRE button. But nothing happened.

"Why isn't Milwaukee eating magma?" Drakken asked, confused.

He hit the button again and again. But it was no use. The Magmamachine was completely clogged with melted Swiss.

Drakken looked down. Cheese was rising around his legs.

"Please, do not tell me that this place is actually made of cheese," he cried. *"I thought it was a cheese-covered building!"*

"Oh, golly, no," said the tour guide, who

floated by on a crate. "You'd be surprised by—" *Gloop*. Before she could finish, a big cheese wave covered her.

Drakken frantically worked the controls, but with no luck. Suddenly, he was sucked into the river of melted cheese.

High above, Kim and Ron climbed into a hole in the wall. They crawled out the other side just in time.

As the cheese wheel collapsed behind them, they heard Drakken scream, "This is not over, Kim Possible!"

And then he was swept away in a current of melted Swiss.

CHAPTER 11

Mission Accomplished

"Drakken's plan is so foiled!" Kim said.

"Oh, it's over," Ron agreed. "I call it 'Bad Guy *con queso*.'"

He stepped back to admire his handiwork. The cheese had cooled off quickly. Now the cheese wheel looked more like a squashed cheesecake. Drakken, Shego, and the henchmen were all stuck in the hardened cheese.

Later, Ron and Kim were back in their usual

spot at Bueno Nacho—in a booth. Ron munched a Naco. Kim sipped a soda and sighed sadly.

"What's wrong, K.P.?" Ron asked. "We won."

"I'm very happy," Kim said. "Really."

"You don't *sound* happy," said Ron.

"Okay," Kim said. "I know this is beyond shallow, but I saved the world, and I'm no closer to owning that Club Banana jacket."

She put her chin in her hand and pouted.

"Maybe," Ron said. "Maybe not."

He reached under the table and pulled out a box. The Club Banana logo was printed on the top.

"Ron?" Kim squealed. She had the best friend in the world! She tore open the box and pulled out the green leather jacket.

Kim held it up. Her green eyes twinkled.

"It's no big deal," Ron said modestly. "My Naco bonus was *muy bueno*."

"You are *too* sweet," she said, hugging the jacket. "I love it!"

Just then, Ned walked up to their table. He had gotten his manager job back. He had on his old green-and-orange manager's shirt and regulation clip-on tie.

And over that, he was wearing a green leather Club Banana jacket.

Kim's and Ron's jaws dropped.

"Ned?" Kim cried in horror.

"Dude, what are you wearing?" asked Ron.

Ned held up a Club Banana catalog picture.

"Somebody left this picture over the cheese machine," he said. "I just *had* to have it." He turned up the collar on his new coat. "*Viva* me!" he exclaimed.

Ron and Kim looked at each other. Then they looked at Kim's new coat. Without a doubt, something had to be done.

"Exchange it?" Ron asked.

"Oh, yeah," Kim said as she threw the jacket back into the box and put the top on tightly.

Wear the same jacket as Ned? As if!